HELPLESS

AT THE GATES OF

GRACELAND

Published by St. Petersburg Press
St. Petersburg, FL
www.stpetersburgpress.com

Original Publication Information:
Wilson, Jon. "Playing Baseball with Jackie Robinson."
Tampa Bay Times. 2006
Wilson, Jon. "The Bout." *Florida Bards: Gulf Coast Poets.* 2020.

Design and composition by St. Petersburg Press and Isa Crosta
Cover and interior illustrations by Justin Groom
Cover design by St. Petersburg Press and Isa Crosta

Paperback ISBN: 978-1-964239-19-4
eBook ISBN: 978-1-994239-20-0

First Edition

HELPLESS

AT THE GATES OF

GRACELAND

JON WILSON

For those who know

HELLO ...

I have always liked to tell stories. It started during my very young years on a farm in far western Nebraska, where I went to a two-room country school. During recess, we played what we called "keepaway," boys against girls. It was a rugby-like game that had no scoring system, but featured a lot of tackling and wrestling as each side tried to "keep away" a ball from the other side. My best friend was Carolyn, a girl my age who was stronger and more athletic. During a fray on our dirt field, I leaped on her back, hoping to knock loose the ball she carried. She bucked me off, dropped the ball, and flattened me with a perfect punch. The game raged on. No one, including me, gave the episode further thought. But the day brought more drama. Carolyn sat directly behind me in our little classroom. We were practicing penmanship when, for some reason, I turned abruptly, leaned, and placed a slurpy kiss on Carolyn's cheek. She scowled, poked her pencil at me, and told the teacher. Our teacher, Mrs. Morris, stood me in a corner until my passion expired in a sea of shame.

Years later, I learned that Carolyn had died far too young. I was surprised at the loss I felt. We hadn't seen each other since third grade. Yet a few minutes in one day left a powerful memory that has endured for decades.

We all have memories that yield stories we could and should tell. Maybe they are buried; if so, dig them up, look them over. Then start writing, and don't think you can't. In fact, don't think at all. Get to your typewriter, your computer screen, your spiral notebook. Let the words come rolling. Let them come from your heart. You will surprise yourself, I guarantee, and you will learn things about yourself.

Most of the settings in this book are in the town where I was born, Scottsbluff, Nebraska, or in St. Petersburg, Florida, where I have lived since 1956. Another setting is in Spain, one of my favorite places to visit. Another is the fanciful burg of St. Petersnoir, where a hard-boiled detective seeks a missing lion.

People have asked whether some of the work herein is autobiographical. Yes, it is. The Jackie Robinson essay is an example. It is true down to the details. Other pieces suggest people, places, and events I've known; some may suggest other elements of my life.

There is a certain amount of what some would call magical thinking. I sometimes toy with time and place. People may roll their eyes; others may understand (or even recognize) the experiences. I have had some myself. It is a curious world we live in.

HELPLESS AT THE GATES OF GRACELAND

I never liked Elvis. Certainly never considered a pilgrimage to his mansion. But Daisy went, and now here I am. Some kind of voodoo, I guess, or maybe guilt. Got me all the way to Memphis from St. Petersburg, Florida. Daisy died and I had to get out. Didn't know what to do, and for some reason I got on a goddamn bus to Tennessee. One way, I told the agent. Those were two of the approximately six words I'd spoken since I'd walked out my front door. Left it unlocked. In my head, *Love Me Tender*. She hadn't been born when Elvis sang it; must have been in 1956 or '57. But she caught onto it somehow and hummed it a lot around the house. "It's us," she told me. "Oh, my darling, I love you," she said, "And I always will." She sang the last four words. Corny. But I would put my arms around her and kiss her forehead, her nose, her lips. I did that even after the accident when I had to identify her. They gave me that pink ribbon she liked to wear in her hair. Dear, dear Daisy, my tender love. I guess that's why I went to Memphis. I had to see what she saw.

***

Took a city bus to the mansion. There were fifteen, twenty people there, mostly women, mostly older. One of them was barefoot. Some wrote notes and attached them to the fence. Another wrote on the sidewalk with thick chalk, pink, Elvis's favorite color. "We love you forever."

***

Saw a guy sitting on an old brown army blanket. He wore a blue blazer, Oxford cloth blue shirt, and khaki trousers folded where his knees should have been. I looked again. The guy had no lower legs. A pair of shined loafers rested beside him.

***

Just a sister fight, I thought. "You're a selfish bitch," Daisy's sister hissed. "I can't handle Mom alone. You are such a bitch!" A fleck of saliva shot past her curling lips. Daisy turned on me. "Can't you stand up for me? Even a little?" She popped my shoulder with the heel of her hand. "You won't stand up for friends. You won't even stand up for me. You are. Such a. Frickin'. Coward!" She yelled the last word. It stunned me. Daisy never lost her temper. Her outburst buried the words I might have used to answer.

It was the last time Daisy touched me. It was the last

time she spoke to me. She cried. She slammed the door behind her. The cop knocked a couple of hours later.

***

The guy with no legs caught me looking at him. He saw
me glance at the polished loafers beside him.

"Reminds me of what I had," he said. His voice was thin
as a dying heartbeat.

He beckoned me closer. "I'm going to heaven or hell.
Which way are ye going?" I couldn't answer. I didn't know.

I asked: "Why here?"

"I wanted to be a marching duck at the Peabody. But
I did not have the feet for it." Surely he joked, perhaps on
two levels. But I saw no hint of a smile. Not even a wink. His
stare grazed the side of my face, vectoring toward infinity.

***

I thought about the guy all day. Where are ye going. The
next morning I caught the first bus to Graceland. The next
day I did the same. I did so the day after. And the next. Always the guy was there, half a man in splendid attire. Sometimes people offered him money. He always turned it down.
"I am certainly not a beggar.

"E has died. E will rise. E will come again," he said.

I walked away. Where are ye going. Couldn't focus,
couldn't think. My knees folded and I stumbled. Where are

ye going. The barefoot woman pointed. "You are lost."

"Aren't we all," I said.

"Who are you? What's your name?"

"I don't know."

***

The guy passed away in the night.

"He did it quiet," the woman said. "No one did a thing to him."

"What about for him?"

"He did it quiet."

She wears the guy's polished loafers. His army blanket remains, a wrinkled, brown wad on the sidewalk. I am certainly not a coward. I straighten the blanket and sit down, half a man in low attire. No one can do a thing for me. I put the pink ribbon beside me. It reminds me of what I had. I gaze at the mansion's bright columns. I say the address out loud: "3467 Elvis Presley Boulevard." I offer the words like a prayer.

She has died.

She will rise.

She will come again.

I love her.

And I always will.

HANGOVER

Death bones rattle
When I drink.
My soul says Goodbye.
At dawn,
Garbage birds
Clatter at my window,
A window dark as dread.

MAGIC
TRICKS

WHO IS CHINA CLARENCE?

China Clarence has dark hair pulled back in a small ponytail. She seems a bit flirtatious. All I want is a soda here in Mister Siglia's shop, but somehow I am compelled to talk.

"How did you get the name China?"

She wears a longish dress, dull blue with thin white vertical stripes, and mules with a smooth, shiny blue vamp. She stands close to me and I notice a sweet scent. It seems to evaporate. Then it comes back. It startles me when China Clarence speaks.

"My dad was in the navy. On some kind of a boat. Did you ever see *The Sand Pebbles*? Like that."

"Wow. So was your mother Chinese?"

"Maybe. Do you have a need to know?"

"I was just curious."

"Let it be a mystery. You shouldn't know too much. It can be dangerous."

I dig out my wallet. I pull a card and thrust it at her.

"Sons of Danger" was printed on it in red letters made to look like they were dripping blood.

"My friend Terry made these. Top adventurer, my hero."

China Clarence looks at the card. She giggles, a sound like wind chimes tinkling. "You are the one," she says. "At last. My danger boy."

She snatches the card and skips away. Her dress's hemline swings. I get a glimpse of a blue slip.

＊＊＊

Mister Siglia runs the only store in town that still sells ice cream sodas. When did they go out of fashion? I ask for them at other places and the counter kids look at me like I've ordered a jelly troutshake.

"Ah, these kids," he says. "They miss the good things in life." One of the good things is a soda by Mister Siglia. He pulls a cold twelve-inch glass out of his chiller, which looks like it is smoking because of the dry ice. Tiny ice drops make the glass sparkle. "Diamond dust," Mister Siglia whispers, his eyebrows bouncing.

He sets the glass on his special counter. There is dry ice underneath it, too. Then he pours in chocolate milk and adds about four squirts of chocolate syrup. "Go light on this stuff," Mister Siglia says. "You don't want it too sweet." He shovels in a hunk of Breyers bigger than his fist. A bottle of club soda follows. "Gives it just a hint of salt, too."

The concoction bubbles to the rim, urgently, almost but not quite spilling over, then recedes. Finally, my favorite part: the whipped cream cylinder hisses a sweet stream, round and round it goes, making a fine white cap on the soda. My life's delight.

***

"So," says Mister Siglia. "You should be careful. She will get you in trouble, that one."

"Do you know her?"

He hands me the soda. He wipes his hands with a white towel. He looks out the window.

"Oh, yes. I know her. So did my father. And my grandfather. And the father before him."

"Wait, how old is she? She looks … kind of young." I look out the window. Maybe I misunderstand.

"You should drink your soda," says Mister Siglia. "Forget about that one."

***

But I could not. I go back for another soda. My second in three days. A bit prodigal, yes, as I usually have a soda just once every few weeks. I am still hungry for one, I tell myself.

Mister Siglia nods as if he knows a secret. I think he looks tired. I watch him squirt the whipped cream. On the third squirt, China Clarence is beside me.

"I want one, too," she says.

"You don't have any money," Mister Siglia says. He does not look at China Clarence. He is not surprised by her presence. He does not look up from his countertop artistry.

"Wait. I'll buy her one," I say. I turn to China Clarence. "I will buy you one. I have money."

"I know you do," she says.

Mister Siglia shakes his head.

***

Three days in a row, I am in Mister Siglia's shop. So is China Clarence.

I summon savoir-faire. Or perhaps not. "Do I know you? Have I seen you before?"

China Clarence smiles as if she expects such questions.

***

On the fourth day, I get my usual soda. I get one for China Clarence.

"I want to dance with you," she says.

"I don't dance much."

"You've been trying to figure out how. With me, right here. You could do more."

Was it an invitation? I couldn't decide.

"I'm just here drinking sodas."

"I know. Sodas are your life. Saturday night go to Jokers."

"That club out by the National Guard? Hasn't been there for years."

"Go to Jokers Saturday night. I'll meet you. Park under that old oak tree. About a block down."

***

I look in my high school yearbooks for pictures of China Clarence. Nothing. So I look for her name on the Internet. Nada. There is something called Clarence China, made in England, teacups, saucers, that sort of thing. That's all.

***

I guess I'm just curious. Saturday night I drive my pick-up to the old Jokers' site. Who is China Clarence? What does she want? Maybe she's bait. Maybe I'm going to get beat up and robbed. Well. I'm a Son of Danger. I see the old oak tree and park under it. I see no Jokers Club. I do see Old Man Garrett's abandoned house on the edge of Clam Bayou. He was a spooky character. He is dead now, but he used to night-walk the woods in a white dress shirt and black suit. He made my friend's wart go away by rubbing it and saying a few weird words, or so I was told. I get out of my truck and lean against the hood. The oak tree seems to sigh. It is a breath in the dark, and I begin to feel uneasy, as if I should be somewhere else.

***

She is not there, and then she is. I flinch just a little. But she projects absolute joy. "I knew you would come," she says. "Dance with me now."

"No music," I say.

"Yes. Over there." China Clarence points and I see the Jokers Club. I do not see how I could have missed it before. I hear a guitar band playing a slow dance, the kind we used to call a grind song. I take China Clarence's right hand in my left and pull it to my shoulder. That delicate aroma hovers about her. My right arm skims around her waist. She glides toward me and for an odd moment I feel as if she is passing through me. She wears a tight black dress. One of her breasts nudges my chest.

Brainy Bertha Jones.

I danced with her once. In high school. She slow-danced the same way, angled in close. Her breath touched my neck. I remember when she whispered. "I do love it so when you hold me close. Don'cha know?"

Odd to recall that just now.

"One dance," China Clarence says. "And what happened later. And then you put up your walls."

She presses in closer. I begin to get a rise.

She whispers. "You told me you were in love."

"We were just kids …"

"I wasn't. Not then, not now," China Clarence says.

"I'm … I really don't understand."

"No need. Go with the flow. That was one thing you were good at."

I hear music from Jokers. *Unchained Melody.* Our song, we used to call it. Bertha and I.

"You have no idea," China Clarence said. "What the mind

can do. You should come with me. I can show you things."

Then: "Come on, Danger Boy. Kiss me."

Our tongues meet, they twist and jab, our teeth collide and rattle. Oh, this kiss. My head spins, I see bright stars, on the ground I see a snake coiling and laughing, its giant mouth grasping my leg, pulling, there is a hole, a hole deep as dark, I tumble and fall forever, and I am not afraid, and I am somewhere, somewhere, somewhere …

***

"What the heck?"

It is sunrise and I lean against a vehicle and it is not my pick-up; it is a blue English Ford, an Anglia model like one I used to have a few years ago. Quite a few years ago, actually. Why am I here? My head doesn't ache. I don't feel sick. I am not hung over. I do not remember sleeping. Heck, what do I remember?

I remember sodas. There was a woman. Kind of an Asian name. I am under an oak tree. It seems to sigh. A zephyr moves its leaves and I catch a hint of … what? Lavender? Yes! She was here! The exotic name, China Clarence. And lavender. Now I remember; that was the scent drifting around her.

"What the heck?"

Did she steal my truck? Leave this old car? I yank the driver's side door. Inside, the long shift stick angles up from the floor. On its end, no shifter grip, the round, white knob to grasp. I run my fingers over the stick's empty threads.

Years ago, a girl, what was her name again, constantly got in my car and stole the knob. Even if I locked the car, she somehow got in and stole the knob. She would only give it back if I promised to drive her to the library.

"What the heck?"

***

There's a key. The Anglia starts right up. Then it jumps and stalls because I forget to use the clutch, been a long time. Do over, now it goes, running like a beauty. I have to get to Mister Siglia's, find out what's going on. I look in the rearview mirror for cops, just like always. I see my hair. Short, that combed down Ivy look. Can't recall getting that haircut. Whatever. Got to get to Mister Siglia's.

***

Mr. Siglia's shop isn't there. There is a store called Martinelz. "Magic Tricks," say the words in its window. I go in. See him.

"Mr. Siglia?"

"My name is Martin Elz," says the man behind the counter.

Am I lost? I go back outside. Look around. Back inside. To Martin Elz: "Do you know Mr. Siglia?"

"Not this time."

Okay. I get it. This is a dream. I know how to get out of

one. I know how to wake myself up.

Then China Clarence stands beside me. I get dizzy. I wish for something I think is real.

"Where's my pick-up?"

"You think I have it?"

"You were there with me, down by Jokers last night."

"How do you know it wasn't someone else?"

"Because I didn't sleep. I didn't talk to anyone else."

"How do you know?"

"What do you mean how do I know? I was awake. All night. Saw the sun come up."

"Weird, huh?"

"Yeah, and that English Ford, where'd you get that?"

"I didn't get it anywhere. It's your car."

"Yeah. Okay. My shift knob's gone, too."

"Just like old time."

"Why, do you have it?"

"Maybe. Maybe I have answers to many of your mysteries."

"How do you even know them? Who are you, anyway?"

China Clarence smiles. "You'll have to come along and see."

"Well, look . . do you want a soda?"

"Not today, thank you."

"How about ... should I drive you to the library?"

"It's a good start."

"Do you want to go right now?"

She smiles.

"In time," she says. "All in a ripple of time."

"Can I get back?"

"There's more to life than sodas, Danger Boy. Don'cha know?"

B
Dodgers
42

PLAYING BASEBALL WITH JACKIE ROBINSON

My first baseball hero played his final game in 1956. Years later, I met Jackie Robinson's daughter at St. Petersburg's James F. Oliver Field.

We stood along the first-base line and chatted, and it seemed to me that Sharon Robinson very much favored her father. Her smile looked like the one I remember from old Brooklyn Dodgers photos taken a half-century earlier.

Jackie Robinson showed me a new world. A 7-year-old farm kid in western Nebraska, I bought a 10-cent comic book about Robinson's baseball career. I read it until its pages came loose.

This was in 1952, pre-Salk vaccine. My schoolmate Gary came down with polio, and it scared parents for miles around. During afternoons, Mom made me stay inside to rest. With nothing much to do, I always turned on the radio. Right after the farm report came Mutual's baseball game of the day, Al Helfer at the mike.

The Dodgers were hot. On a farm 2,000 miles away, I

got hooked on Pee Wee, Gil, Duke, Campy, and especially No. 42. I tried to emulate him. During the evening's cool, I stood with a bat cocked over a No. 10 tin can, crushed flat for a home plate. Sometimes I'd toss my baseball and whack it. My best hits rattled into the feed trough of our cattle pen.

Poking up a few miles away was Chimney Rock, an Oregon Trail landmark. But I saw myself in Brooklyn's Ebbets Field. "Swung on, a hard drive to left-center, another base-hit." I imagined Helfer calling the play-by-play. Wanting to be fast like Jackie, I practiced stealing bases. Sliding in a farmyard always amounted to a precarious adventure.

I was aware Robinson looked different than I, but I had no idea about the depth of history or the meaning of skin color. His comic-book biography glossed the ugly parts of breaking Major League Baseball's color barrier in 1947.

I liked my Uncle Joe, a barber. He was a sports fan and cracked jokes. If you had a slingshot, he was more interested in helping you aim correctly than warning you about putting a rock through someone's retina.

But he snorted at a young relative who favored the Dodgers. It was clear that Robinson was one of the reasons behind his attitude. It also was an early clue that life was more complicated than learning to be part of a double-play combination at second base. It was years before I understood what Robinson had endured during his career. Racial references flew over my head.

Come World Series time, I hid out in a closet at Fairview #50, our country school. My friend Carolyn brought a little radio. We crouched among the coats, wearing what passed as our baseball gloves. The mitts were 1930s vintage, flat, misshapen things barely bigger than the hands they were supposed to cover. We sat there popping our fists into the leather, hanging on the game's every pitch. Carolyn giggled every time the announcer mentioned the name Campanella, the Dodgers' catcher.

The Dodgers didn't win a Series until 1955. I was home for lunch and saw it on our new television set. After the last game's last out, I ran back to school, shouting all the way, eager to make fun of my friends who liked the New York Yankees.

The Dodgers and Yanks went at it again in 1956. This time the World Series came through the static-rattled car radio of our 1953 Ford. We were chasing the Florida dream. Somewhere on U.S. Highway 40 in Ohio, I heard Jackie take his last at-bat ever. He struck out to end game seven.

Soon, he retired. The Dodgers moved to Los Angeles. My family settled in St. Petersburg. Life changed. I don't know how much my childhood adulation of Jackie Robinson influenced my attitudes while growing up and older in a Southern city. A facile judgment won't work. But meeting Sharon Robinson somehow completed a connection. I told her part of the story.

Ever gracious, she said she had never heard one quite like it. I didn't get everything out. Something caught in my throat, and I had to hush. Time's gravity, perhaps life's intricacy, can descend suddenly, carrying emotions. I wanted

to tell her that I have never forgotten her father. And to say
I have never forgotten those few years when Jackie Robinson introduced me to baseball, opened my imagination,
and played the invisible teammate in a dusty, high-plains
farmyard.

HIGH PLAINS HARVEST

First-graders learning to scissor
Turn to the last open window.
They notice a new perfume.
Leaves burning, brown and orange
Like country-school cut-outs.

Then Saturday: We blow our breaths in puffs,
Hear the distant crump of guns.
Hunters kick through dry ditches
And startle pheasants and shoot.
Bare cornstalks lay pale.
Night frost has scrubbed the soil bright.
We walk a beet field newly stripped,
Its dirty hard roots sent to be spun to gold.
A bonfire, a circle, loud men
Drink beer out of bottles, an accordion
Pumps a polka. The men dance alone.

I think of a picture book.
I ask: Are they witches?
Daddy laughs. Sugar tramps, he says,
Then he laughs some more. Witches!
And so I laugh, too, or at least
That kind of noise drops out of my mouth
Into the tilt-a-whirl shadows.

At home, on my floor, my skeleton,
First prize, best costume.
The pale bones I kick under the bed.
In the dark
The coal train's night whistle
Whines at my window.
I think of the witches.
I laugh like I might laugh forever.

JESUS UP THE CREEK

I'd done my work at the blacksmith shop, ten hours straight, dead tired, and Mister Binnie told me to get out before I set my wooden leg on fire. His parting words went as usual, something about me being so ugly that I was scaring the horses. He didn't mean much by it, and it was what half the people in St. Petersburg thought anyway, but it was hurtful all the same. They called me Leg when they thought I wasn't listening.

But things changed because of Booker Creek, down where it courses through a little valley in Roser Park. I heard someone call that ravine a thin place, meaning a place where the veil between worlds is easily penetrated. Please contemplate that thought before you dismiss the next few words as fiction.

I'd gotten a buggy ride down there with Mister Charles Roser's hired man. I stretched out on a hillside, unusual in St. Pete, safe under the arms of a giant oak. People said it must have sprouted when the Tocobagas were here. I could shut my eyes, go back in time, and be with them. They'd be fixing a canoe or throwing a stick so a dog could go splashing into the creek after it, and they'd laugh. Sometimes I talked to them, like anyone might do with their neighbors. Once in a while, they seemed to hear, and they'd look around like they'd heard a voice come up from the ground. They didn't seem surprised, but they'd never answer.

I came for peace that day. You know what I mean. There's no place like it in St. Pete. A little cooler, even in August, the creek swishing along, maybe an otter in it, maybe a brave little breeze sneaking around the trees.

Except the Adventists were whooping it up by the streetcar bridge. They had a camp, looked like enough tents for General Lee's blessed gray army, and they were having outdoor prayer meetings three times a day.

And a storm was coming.

West of town boiled a purple-black cloud. It was throwing down lightning that looked like hot spikes, and underneath it, gray rain hammered. The creek was building and flowing faster.

I thought about finding a way to leave. If I had to walk, it would take a while because of my leg, and to tell you the truth, it hurt if I had to go far.

Then that urchin showed up out of nowhere. He had a double-dare look in his eyes and a smart mouth.

"Name's Johnny Floyd Delaney and I got some devil bones," he told me. "You shoot any craps?"

"Naw."

"Well, I figured as much. You from that Bible crowd over there?"

"Naw."

I waited for him to say I was ugly, but he didn't.

"Go ahead, ask. Get it over with," I said.

"Ask what?"

"About my leg. My face. A boat blew up and I got hurt. So."

He didn't say a word, just stared into space. His double-dare look went away. We could hear something up the creek. It sounded like the big faucet on Mister Binnie's rain barrel when he let the water out.

Then Johnny Floyd Delaney said, "Look at these." He pulled a whole string of Hitt's Thunder Flashcrackers out of his pocket. Three inches long, every one of them.

I looked him over. He wore a sailor suit with blue stripes on the collar, a blue anchor stitched in. He barely reached my chest, and I wasn't very tall. He had bird's-nest hair dark as dirt and odd eyes the color of tea.

I asked him: "How old are you, anyway? About eight?"

"Yeah, like the stork, Santa Claus, and Yahweh live in Saint George Washington's cherry tree."

"Huh?"

"Huh? Huh? You sound like one of those chippies trying to make you think you're doing her good."

He made me want to punch him, but heck. He was just a little bird chirping away. Or so I thought. Besides, we had a bad storm coming. Up the stream, that faucet sound was louder. I looked toward the Adventists and wondered if they heard it. Now and then, a storm made Booker Creek swell up and go rampaging toward Tampa Bay like a huge wave swallowing tree limbs, bicycles, maybe half of somebody's front porch, and more than once the body of some luckless soul caught unaware by the power of the surge.

"I'm sixteen," Johnny Floyd Delaney said. "You haven't been where I've been."

"Oh, I've been around. I'm seventeen. Been over to Tampa. Been to Clearwater. Took a steamer up to Cedar Key. Anyway, y'know what? I think it's going to flood. Right over the banks. Fast."

"Come on," said Johnny Floyd Delaney. "Let's go over there and throw some bangers at all those preachers."

He took off running. I followed, thumping along on my leg. It hurt. A lightning spear ripped so close I heard it sizzle, and I felt a little shock, and I cringed, waiting for the thunder blast. It never came.

But I saw Johnny Floyd Delaney charge the Adventists and throw his Flashcrackers at them. How he got that string lit I'll never know. But I heard them popping like rifle shots and I saw the camp meeting come apart. A few people started running.

I took off running like the wind, but I wasn't as fast as Booker Creek. I saw it flash flood from the corner of my eye, and it was a roaring cascade, not a friendly stream. I saw the little guy in the sailor suit stop dead. I caught up with him.

"Bend down," he said, looking up at me. I did, and he kissed me right on the lips. Then he backed toward the flood.

"Now you're a hotsie-totsie," he said.

He fell backward, arms spread wide. I reached for him but could only tear a piece off his sailor-suit collar. He hit the water and went under.

"No!" I yelled. "Swim! You can swim out!"

But he was gone. All that was left was the piece of bright white cloth I'd torn, swirling on top of the foam.

I had a flashing thought. I could follow him and put to rest all my sadness. But my foot … it tingled. Like it had gone to sleep and was coming back.

"Jesus Christ Almighty! My foot! My two feet!"

I stumbled up the bank and looked down, and I had my boot on one foot and the other was bare, and I had a leg that looked muscular and strong. And I … had run. I fell on the ground and sobbed. I knew I'd wake up and still have that damned wooden leg.

But I didn't, and I felt my face, and the flesh was smooth with no scars and burns. It terrified me. Maybe I was dead. I bawled. I felt a hand on my shoulder, pulling. I thought it must be the constable.

"Son, you will mount up with wings of eagles."

No constable I knew talked like that.

The Adventists thought I threw the Flashcrackers. They looked up from their hymnals. They saw the flood. They got away. They didn't see a little kid in a sailor suit.

They called me a hero.

***

I eventually left the blacksmith shop and married young Jenny of the temperance ladies. The Adventists put up a church near their old camp. I started building bungalows in Roser Park, and my bride and I moved into one.

I never told anyone but Jenny about that strange day, and she just smiled and kissed my cheek. It's odd how no one ever asked me how come I had two good legs again and no scars, as if they had never known me otherwise.

I never figured out much about that day. But I was still drawn to Booker Creek's ravine, the thin place where I had talked to the Tocobagas and, through devilry or divination, found myself made whole.

One day I came home from a walk there and found a music box on the front steps. Where it came from, I could not say. Old and exquisite, it had a violin and floral arrangements inlaid on its cover. I opened it. It played *Shall We Gather at the River*.

It also contained a torn piece of white cloth with a little blue anchor stitched in the middle.

Johnny Floyd Delaney.

I guess he was saying hello from the other side of the veil. I wasn't surprised.

LYRIC FOR LOVE

I think of me and you
On our burly dreamland steed,
Riding hard, the emerald turf
A-thunder under slate and azure sky
Near our cliffs, near our Dooneen.

All in forest green
You ride. I fancy
Your cape a-billow like a flag,
Reins flashing in your fists.
My arms around your little waist.

I press my ear upon your back.
I hear your heart's canter.
I feel its leap
When we touch the banks of heaven
Near the cliffs of our Dooneen.

THE LADY AND THE LION
TALES FROM ST. PETERSNOIR, OCTOBER, 1948

By Stag Majors

(As told to Jon Wilson)

I'd just met a pixie, but I canned the small talk and got right to the point.

"So what's this missing lion look like?"

"He's beige. Bushy mane. Yellow eyes. Long tail, big paws."

I took careful notes and kept firing razor-sharp questions.

"Any identifying marks?"

"Well, he doesn't have tattoos, if that's what you mean."

"Got a name?"

"Iris O'Holladay, I already told you."

I loved hearing her say it, so I didn't crack wise.

"I'm talkin' about this king of the beasts you said you lost."

"He's not gonna come if you call him."

This time I couldn't help it. I gave with the eye roll. I sighed in my patient way.

"Look, lady. I really wanna help. There's cabbage in it for me, like you promised. If I can do you a favor too, it's egg in my beer."

I must have hurt her feelings. Miss O'Holladay—I didn't

see any wedding rings— burst into tears. For someone so tiny, she had lot of water stored up, and she could sob like a Seaboard locomotive.

"I'm ... I'm so sorry. It's just ... I'm so worried about Pounce."

"He wouldn't hurt anybody. He's just a big sweetie. I named him Pounce on account of how he jumps on his little teddy. He can't even tear it up; he's so old most of his teeth are gone, and they took his claws off ages ago. I just want him safe. Before one of those men shoots him between the eyes with a Tommy gun."

Well, it figured.

I could just hear the cops yakking, flicking cigarette ashes, and drinking their warmed-up joe. Yeah, remember Stag Majors? Used to be the top private eye in St. Petersnoir. Now he's chasing a washed-up lion.

Pounce da Lion, the toothless terror. I could see the headline now. Little did I know. Before the afternoon rag hit the streets, the lady and the lion would change my life. But of course, I'm ahead of the story.

***

It all started about 30 minutes earlier. Six a.m. and I was chain-smoking Luckies like it was D-Day and I was swilling joe to make me sleep. And if you think that's a load of nonsense, you should see the rest of my life. I needed the mazumah in a big way. Even my dandruff was yelling for a few squares. And the morning *Times* sports section— Jeezoos

Jasper, what a disaster. I wanted inside dope on Army-Notre Dame, and all the mullet wrap gives me was this Green-Devils-St. Pete-Will-Shine bushwa.

I mean, I gotta give St. Pete High credit. They probably won the state championship beating Jacksonville Landon the way they did, running that way when the whole state figured they'd run this way. Misdirection. Works every time, unless you bump up against somebody really shifty.

But Friday night was history. It was Saturday morning. I needed some new low-down—up high and quick.

And I was about to need a whole lot more.

In those days I had what passed for an office in the Crislip Arcade down on Central. It was just me most of the time. If I was really flush, I'd have a girl in to answer the phone and smile at me. At the moment, I wasn't really flush. Nobody was smiling and I was wondering if I had the moxie to spend my last two bits on a bolita ticket. It couldn't make things much worse.

Then they got worse. I heard him coming. Those big rope-soled shoes of his slapped the arcade floor like mullet falling off a roof, whacking, echoing, a relentless advancing nightmare. And sure enough, DeLyle Wilpole Jr. himself crashed through my door like all the junk out of Fibber McGee's closet.

"Smile at me, Wilpole. I need a friend." I whistled a few lines of *Oh What a Pal Was Whoozis.*

Wilpole was pale as an egg and as yellow inside. But he was loyal as a chigger. Plus he always had a good tip on the dogs at Derby Lane—if you could snag it out of the two dozen he dished every week.

It was 6:10 a.m. and I could see he was passionate.

"Didja see it? Didja see it in the newspaper? Omigolly, ya gotta see it, quick, turn the page!"

Another thing about Wilpole was, he had epizootics of the blowhole.

But I lamped the headline on the sports section's lead story:

Green Devils Cage Lions

it said in big, dark letters, and there was a smaller headline right under it:

Visitors' Mascot Flees Stewart Field

"Well, hot wallop, Wilpole, I was that kid from Landon, I'd flee, too. Thirty-five to fourteen, c'mon. I shoulda bet."

"Ixnay, boss, look at the front page!"

"I ain't your boss, Wilpole."

But I riffled the rag until page one showed up—and there it was in VJ Day type:

Lion Loose In City
Officials Urge Stay Inside

The newspaper story went like this:

"Jacksonville Landon's live lion mascot burst out of its cage during the football game with St. Petersburg High School last night, sparking a massive hunt through all sections of the city. At press time, no attacks had been reported. There was no sign of the lion, which police chief Jake Reichert said may have escaped to a wooded area west of the football field on Ninth Avenue North.

"There were unconfirmed sightings reported from the Goose Pond, from Roser Park, and from as far north as Pinellas Park, where locals were said to be armed.

"Chief Reichert urged calm and pleaded for residents to stay indoors until the animal is killed or captured. Nearly one hundred officers, county deputies, highway patrol troopers and game wardens have been pressed into the hunt. Governor Caldwell offered to send National Guard troops ..."

"Whaddya think, Wilpole? Is he gonna come downtown, bite some Republicans?"

"No, no, boss! You missed the best part! Look at the bottom!"

My eyes tumbled down the column. "The lion's owner is offering a $500 reward if the animal is returned unharmed ..."

My eyes bugged like a stomped-on catfish's.

Five hundred simoleons! The thought made my head spin.

I didn't even hear the phone go off.

Wilpole said: "You gotta cut me in, boss, okay?" Then he unhorsed the yacker and handed it over.

Thirty seconds later, I was sprinting to the Princess Martha Hotel, dodging the No. 2 trolley on its first run of the day down First Avenue. Funny. I thought I heard the *Notre Dame Victory March* drifting on the bay breeze.

Made me think of a circus somehow.

*****

Triple deuces was the Princess Martha room number. A little doll answered the door. She had honey hair and eyes like clear October sky.

"My, you're so tall!" she purred.

"For you I'll try to be shorter," I said, gazing down from my towering 5 feet 6.

She couldn't have stretched more than 4 feet 9 in her pink patent pumps. She had on a pinafore to match and a rosy stickum that turned her lips to liquid candy. Three seconds at her door and my strings were humming.

She put the kibosh on that, but quick.

"Don't be a smart aleck," she told me. "And don't get any funny ideas. I'm all business, buster."

"You can call me Majors," I said. "Stag Majors, private eye. You the one with the real gone cat?"

Iris O'Holladay said she used to dress up in a red ballet costume and crack whips at lions and tigers in a traveling sideshow. Then she mistimed a stroke and snapped out an old male's eye. The show's owner put the codger down rather than pay a vet bill. Ever since, Iris had been trying to make it up by being nice to big animals that could eat people.

I wanted to flex my muscles, stand on tiptoe, and show my teeth.

"Iris O'Holladay, heart like a hot scoop a Dairy Queen, huh?"

A magic line. Works every time.

Iris's baby blues washed me up and down and in and out and everywhere else all over.

"I believe in you, Stag Majors. Somebody made me believe in you. I heard you stay on the job and satisfy your clients."

My head started swimming again.

But I stayed on the job.

"What's Pounce's story, Miss O'Holladay?"

She said she'd adopted him when she left the carnie life. The two of them settled down. Pounce even had his own room. He could have lived out his days in elderly lionish bliss.

Except that Iris had graduated from Jacksonville Landon. And this year, the Lions thought they had the best football team in the state. St. Pete High argued about it. It took the gamblers in Tampa to arrange a game.

"I thought it would be fun to let the kids borrow Pounce. You know, for school spirit. I'd get to come along. I made the arrangements for his trip and a nice cage. I thought it would be like being back in school again.

"Except this time, I'd have my own lion!"

She looked so wistful that I had to look down at my shoes, which was a bad idea. They were cracked and scuffed and they made me feel like a bum.

I got back on the job with a point-blank question. "Where would a lion go in St. Petersnoir, Miss O'Holladay?"

"Do you have jungles here? That's where he'd go. Some place far away. Where he could hide and nobody could find him."

Yeah. I dug it. Me and Pounce thought the same way.

Only thing is, I couldn't think of what street he'd take to Nowhereville. And I'd been down plenty of 'em. Sometimes on all fours, too.

But I knew somebody who might dope it out.

He knew every street and alley in St. Petersnoir, and every wet footprint on every Augusta brick.

He was the boss of the Fourth Street Lords.

✳✳✳

The Lords played with switchblades, ran numbers for north side guys, and rolled square kids for their movie money downtown. None of 'em had seen their eighteenth birthday, and most would be lucky to see a twentieth.

Jacksie Crudup called the shots.

Jacksie lived in a lean-to nailed to the Eight Ball, a sleazy bar on a dirt-and-garbage alley.

I pounded on a tattered screen door and bleated a mouth-bugle reveille. "Rise and shine, sweetheart, your fan club awaits!"

"Am-scray, copper, it's Saturday. Anyways, I'm sixteen and I don't gotta go to your lousy schools no more."

"It ain't the hooky cop, Jacksie, it's your old pal Stag Majors, private eye. You got that lion in there? Either you step out here or I'm comin' in full automatic."

"Ah, ya'll shoot yer foot off, ya busted-up old has-been. Just hold yer horses."

A while back, I'd pulled Jacksie out of a scrape with the Spanish Knights in Tampa. I figured he owed me.

But he was ornery as they come. At night he gulped the beer the Eight Ball barflies left. He washed the glasses for nickels. He stole the barmaid's tips. It was steady work for a junior high dropout.

I got tired of waiting and kicked the door, breaking the flimsy latch and knocking out the bottom screen.

Jacksie was sitting on old Army cot with an inch-thick mattress and one oily sheet. He was lighting a cigar butt and looked like he'd been sleeping off a drunk.

"Thanks, dingbat, I hope yer gonna hang around to kill the flies."

"Good to see you, too, Jacksie. Tell me about this lion that got loose, and give it to me straight. I can still point you out to those Tampa guys."

Jacksie smirked. He sucked on the butt and got some heat going. The thing smelled like it was stuffed with shreds of fried jock strap. "So, this so-called lion. He worth anything?"

"Could be. How about not having Tampa cut you a dumb smile below the one you already got."

I could almost hear Jacksie's brain, such as it was, grinding out the possibilities.

"They was small. I thought it was a bunch of grade-school squirts. Like those twerps that run around under the goalposts after the game? Except these guys looked kinda strong for their size. Looked like they knew the score, too."

I asked: "How many?"'

"Musta been four, five. They just put a rope around its … hey! You wanna know any more, you're gonna have to lay the loot."

I hated to tell Jacksie the spondulix and me weren't well acquainted at the moment.

He said: "Yeah, well, maybe I ain't well acquainted with what happened next about that lion. Hey! You know what they call them organ things that play circus music?"

"Calliopes. Why?" (And what was that little itch in the back of my mind?)

"Well, when they was takin' the lion, one of them calliopes come blazin' down Twenty-Fourth Street, clear the other side of the field. Everyone goes runnin' over? Whish! These little guys sneak up, they get the lion, nobody sees 'em. Except me. And Simpy Moran."

Then he clammed up, got up, walked into a broom closet, and slammed the door.

"Hey Jacksie! You sure nobody else saw anything?" I heard a toilet flush in the broom closet.

"Nah. We was under the stands. Waitin' fer some dummy with dough to come along? You know. And they was all over tryin' to see that dumb calliope. Like it was some dumb circus in town.

"Now beat it, Majors. I got a headache."

When Jacksie was done, Jacksie was done. The only way to keep him yakking was to lay the lettuce on him, and I didn't have the groceries.

I shoved out the door, yanking loose a hinge. I was standing in the alley wondering what to do next when Jacksie shouted one more thing.

"Go find Simpy. He's the one followed 'em."

I pushed the hinge screws back in the wood. One little favor deserves another.

Simpy Moran was thirteen and still let dry snot hang on his lip. This morning the stuff was mixed with dry blood. Someone had given him a real broderick.

I found him gasping in the dead-end alley behind the Detroit Hotel, where the Lords had a shack they used for meetings. Simpy looked so bad I wondered if he was going to make it.

"Dey was little guys … Mean," he gasped. "Dey caught me spyin' on 'em. Beat me bad. I t'ink dey busted me up inside, my gut hurts somethin' awful."

"Take it easy, Simpy, we'll get ya fixed up. Where'd this happen?"

"Dey got a hide-out. Delmar Terrace. Over by da West Coast Inn …" Simpy started retching.

The poor little squirt. I felt sorry for him. His so-called folks were from New Jersey or Brooklyn, some kind of place like that, and they dumped him in St. Petersnoir a year ago. It came out "Mistah Majuhs" when he talked to me.

"Simpy, listen. We'll get you fixed up, but you gotta tell me. I'm lookin' for that lion they had. Did you see what they did with it?"

"I saw 'em shut him up in Little Saint Mary's, Mistah Majuhs. Dey put out a toilet busted sign and locked him in theah. Mistah Majuhs, I need to see a Holy Fodda. I t'ink I'm dyin'."

"Ah, no, yer not, Simpy. Listen to me. Whaddya mean they was short guys?"

"Little bigger dan dose guys in da *Wizahd of Oz*. But real strong. And dey was mean, Mistah Majuhs. Dey got real mad when I tried t'play on that screechy piana a theirs. Anyway, dey're robbin' a bank, somethin' like dat."

I had to think and think hard. I should be good with nonsense. Story of my life, remember? So a bunch of short guys boost a lion out of a high school football game. They lock him in a public restroom.

They beat up a thirteen-year-old with a little kid's snotty lip. Why, I oughta …

Then I think again.

It's 7:30 Saturday morning. I got a line on Pounce. That means I got a line on five hundred simoleons. So what is the hold-up?

Which reminded me, which is one of the beauties of thought.

"Simpy. Whaddya mean they're robbin' a bank or something? Simpy? Hey. Simpy?"

The squirt'd passed out. Or so I figured. I put my ear on his ratty shirt to listen for a beat. His b.o. about made me pass out. I heard his ticker. At least I thought I did. I figured I better make some phone calls.

I went through Simpy's pockets and found two nickels. The first one I used to call triple deuces at the Princess Martha.

"This is Iris O'Holladay …"

My head started swimming. I wanted to ask her if she still had on that pinafore. I wanted to ask if she still believed in me. I wanted her to say her name one more time.

But I stayed on the job. I said:

"I know where your lion is."

Iris O'Holladay squealed. Funny. I couldn't tell if she was overjoyed or just surprised.

"Is he ... alive? Did anyone hurt him?"

The fact wasn't lost on me that Iris O'Holladay was short and so were the eight-balls who boosted a lion, slugged a thirteen-year-old, and were getting ready to do a rob job.

I mentioned the coincidence.

Iris started bawling again. "I know who they are," she squawked. "They're the Horrible Willises. They are cut-throats and animal killers. I left their carnie, and they hate me for it.

"They must have followed me here! They stole Pounce so all the police would chase him and they could go rob those poor men in the armored car! I know it!"

She was really getting wound up, and she was saying things that made my head hurt. She knew more than a thing or two about those short guys. And what about an armored car? Simpy said a bank.

Maybe Iris O'Holladay knew a thing or two more.

But I let it go. I turned off the questions. I didn't want Iris blowing town, now that she owed me.

"Look, Miss O'Holladay, your lion's fine. I'll get all this settled. Then what say we take in a movie? *Easter Parade*'s on at La Plaza."

I figured dames are sweet on Fred Astaire, and Garland's

grown up since her Dorothy days. Plus I wanted some time alone with Miss Pinafore.

I told her we could catch the matinee and that I'd pick her up in the mezzanine lounge at the Princess. I hung up and dropped the other nickel to call my old pal Scanlon, ace reporter, better known as Scoop, at the *Evening Independent.*

It was 8:44 a.m. He picked up the phone on half a ring.

"This is Scanlon, what's the scoop?"

"Hold on to your hat, I got the lion, I got a robbery, I got a story."

"And I got sixty-one minutes 'til deadline, jughead, so talk fast."

I machine-gunned the facts. Lion locked. Little Saint Mary's. Cover to rob a bank. Gang of short guys.

He covered the receiver with his hand and I heard his muffled shout.

"Stop the presses, we got a lead on the lion!"

Then he was back on the yacker, but I could barely hear him. There was a loud plane revving its engine over at Albert Whitted Airport.

"The big cat's news," Scanlon said. "But you're late on the heist. A bunch of little guys blew the back off an armored car, kayoed the guard, and grabbed the loot. Mighta been fifty grand. Reichert's goin' nuts."

Sure he was. All the chief's cops, out chasing a lion which has no fangs, no claws, and which was doing nothing but playing long-tailed space heater on a men's room floor two minutes from the cop shop.

And Iris O'Holladay knew about the armored car.

I was trying to dope it out, and hoping I was wrong, but that roaring, revving airplane made it hard to think.

All of a sudden, a hunch fell on my head like Tantor the Elephant. "Kreegah!" I shouted. Then I clued Scanlon.

"Get yer keister to the airport, but quick. Yer gonna get a story, win ya one a them Poolitzers. Just put my name in the headline, okay?"

I started to hang up and remembered one more thing: "And get an ambulance to the Detroit. There's a kid beat up bad about to croak. By the old blacksmith shop."

I slammed the yacker and took off running, primed to pump lead. Sometimes October makes life worth living.

***

I sprinted east past Mastry's and the Greydog station, and by the time I turned south at the Chatterbox, I was wheezing like a busted Hoover and my ticker was banging like a cannon. Too many Luckies and too much hooch, worth every puff and swig, but now I needed the gas.

I could hear the airplane revving, and it was music to my hunch.

The short guys had to scram. Quickest way out of downtown, one the cops wouldn't figure? Over the water. Take a boat.

Or maybe a plane.

Albert Whitted was six blocks away. Then it was five. Four. I was no Citation, and I was ready to woof my cookies. But I was just about there. The engine bellowed. Then I saw it.

A monoplane, one of those hot old jobs like Wiley Post's, four-hundred-and-fifty horses. And the little guys were getting ready to pile in.

I pulled my beanshooter and fired off a round just for grins. "Kreegah! Bundolo!" The engine drowned my shouts, but I was charging like the cavalry.

They saw me bearing down and scattered like a rack of pool balls. One, two, three, five, how many, for cripes sake?

"Halt! Stop dead!" I shouted, hammering off another round at nothing in particular.

The short guys quit moving. Their eyes flickered this way and that.

I told them: "Turn off that airplane! Lay on the ground! Hand over the money!"'

And then I went kicks over keister.

It was the oldest trick in the book. One of the little guys I didn't see bent down behind me. Two in front of me leaped like cats, knocking me backward. My duff smacked the dirt and my gat went spinning. One of the little shysters snatched it. He jammed it in my ear.

"Youse a dead man, Alley Oop," he squealed.

I closed my eyes and waited for the curtain.

Then a whirlwind on wheels broke up the party.

***

I cracked open one eye. At first I thought it was Scoop Scanlon roaring up on a motorcycle, one of those Indian Scouts. But then the rider jumped off, one hand pointing a gun, the other waving a big shiny badge.

"Federal agent! Drop the gun and drop on the ground! All of you!"

The airplane revved and started rolling.

Blam! Blooie! Two shots from the agent's gun, two plane tires flat as a street cop's feet.

It took me two seconds to shake the flinches. I looked at the agent. I did a double take. Then a triple.

It was another short guy! No, it wasn't a guy! It was … Iris O'Holladay?

But no patent pumps and pink pinafore. She had on high-topped tennis shoes, black slacks, a Boston Braves sweatshirt, and a baseball cap, which was hiding all that honey hair.

She got down to business quick.

"My name is Federal Agent Madge Brakeley, and you are under arrest for stealing interstate bank shipments, theft of an aircraft, and transporting wild animals across state lines without a license."

It was 9:14 a.m. and I stayed on the job.

"Yeah! And for beating up snot-nosed kids for no reason!" I yelled and pointed my gat, which I'd grabbed back in all the chaos.

About that time, Madge Brakeley's back-up arrived. Two big guys in a panel truck.

"Zip your lip, Majors," Federal Agent Madge said. "And put that weapon away."

I did as I was told and watched the two huskies load six crooks— including a pilot—into the van.

Turned out, there were supposed to be seven.

"Where's Wild Card?" Madge snarled.

Nobody answered. But a calliope's sound came drifting on the wind.

"Wild Card Willis," Madge said. "He never knows when to stop."

She yanked up the Indian Scout and swung aboard.

And then I saw Scoop Scanlon flooring his rattling jalopy across the airfield. I never could figure why these newspaper guys didn't drive better cars.

He slammed to a stop and almost tore off a door leaping out. "What's the scoop?" he shouted.

It was 9:20 a.m.

Madge looked at Scanlon, then nodded at me.

"He'll tell you the whole story," she said. "He's the hero here."

Then she kick-started the Scout and tore toward the blare of the calliope.

I watched Madge humming out of sight, the van and her huskies following.

The hero here, she'd called me.

Yeah. That and a nickel gets me a cuppa joe at the Owl Diner.

"Hey!" yelled Scanlon. "I gotta find a phone! Get in the

car! Gimme the scoop!"

I told him how October had once held such promise.

∗∗∗

Scanlon made his deadline. He did me proud. The afternoon headline read:

Local private eye nabs lion, foils heist

Front page stuff, too.

The story was all about me chasing clues, solving the mystery of the missing lion, and oh, by the way, catching a gang and saving the entire St. Petersnoir tourist season.

Seems the armored car carried the hotel association's mazumah to get things moving when the November snowbirds came to town.

Anyway, that's what Paul Davis said in his column. Even Jeff Moshier, the sports editor at Scanlon's paper, put in his two bits: "Stag Majors saved this city's bacon," he wrote. "Opinion here is, they should name a dog after him at Derby Lane."

It was all great, but ...

Name a dog?

Name the meals I'd miss meantime.

I checked my mailbox at the Open Air. Empty as my future.

I plodded across First Avenue, nothing to do, no place to go. I spent my last two bits buying a poppy from the blind guy. Why not, it was almost Armistice Day. I wandered into the mezzanine lounge at the Princess.

And there she was, almost like she was waiting. Not quite the wailing frail, but not quite Madge the Badge, either.

She had on a gabardine suit cut to every curve and that rosy stickum back on her lips.

"I guess you figured out I'm plain clothes, confidential, strictly on the QT," Iris O'Holladay-Madge Brakely said.

I kept my mouth shut, my ears open, and my eyes on those sky-blues she was still flashing.

Madge— not Iris—told me she'd gone undercover with the Horrible Willises a couple of years ago. She worked in their carnival, winning them over, riding motorcycles with them, round and round, on the Wall of Death show. "You have to be small for that," she said.

"And kind of crazy."

Well, they loved her. So it was easy for her to talk them into the lion caper.

That was the misdirection.

That and the calliope.

Madge knew every cop in town would go chase the man-eater. She knew Wild Card Willis would keep playing his screeching calliope to lure any rubes left downtown when the armored car came in. Same idea when Madge made sure the paper had that business about a five-hundred-dollar reward. Get everybody gone, off the streets, on the chase.

Misdirection.

Even yours truly was part of the game. Madge wanted to make sure someone kept tabs on Pounce. She'd run into

Wilpole while casing the Jockey Club and he dropped my name. All unbeknownst to yours truly, of course.

Just like I did, the Horrible Willises bought all of it. They thought Madge—uh, Iris—was on their side.

Turned out, she was on mine. First, she dumped the publicity on me. She said she couldn't use it. "I'm strictly confidential, on the QT, down low," she said.

Then she dropped a double sawbuck on me and said I'd be hearing more from Uncle Sam. I hoped that didn't mean he was going to tax me for the twenty.

Then she stood on tiptoe and planted a smacker on my cheek.

"It was nice knowing you, big boy," she purred.

I wanted to beat my chest and yodel like the Lord of the Jungle.

But all I did was wave bye-bye as she walked away.

Wilpole was waiting when I got back to the office. He had a stack of the afternoon papers and the new Tarzan comic book. I grabbed it and started reading. Wilpole also had a pile of phone messages.

"I thought I told you not to answer the phone when you're in here."

"Boss, boss, boss," he said, "You gotta look at em, they're all good news, you're famous, you might even be rich. I got an interest in seeing you do the right thing, we might even make the big time, we …"

Like I said. Epizootics of the blowhole.

"Wilpole," I said, "There's no we in this office. Not when

you're the other party."

But this time he was onto something.

The hotel association and the chamber of commerce called to say they were going to fatten my bank account for saving theirs.

The Be Kind to Animals Society had a reward for finding the lion. The feds were going to reward me for helping their agent. Yeah, and the Derby Lane people said there would be a Stag Majors running in the season-opener.

Maybe he'd be a winner.

Just like me. It looked like I'd be on Easy Street for a while.

I even felt good about handing Wilpole a cut, and I figured I'd do the same for Jacksie Crudup.

In a few days, they dismissed poor little Simpy Moran from Mound Park Hospital. After I paid his bill, natch.

And Pounce, well, I got him an easy job at the Wild Animal Ranch out on Fourth Street. It was a big relief to the patrons of Little St. Mary's, let me tell ya.

Wild Card Willis remained at large. He's probably still playing the calliope somewhere, and I guess Madge is still chasing him.

All copacetic except for the guys at the police station, flicking their cigarettes and drinking their warmed-up joe. Look at this guy, they said. Catch a lion with no teeth, run in a bunch of short guys, and he thinks he's some kinda J. Edgar Hoover, they said.

I had to educate them.

First thing, a lion is a lion. Period.

And the next thing is, don't tell me little guys aren't tough.

"You ever heard of that Ponce de Leon? Spanish guy found Florida? Wore armor and sailed all over the place? Got in fights with everybody he saw? 4-foot-11, that's what he was. And all those tough guys he bossed? They weren't even that big. "

"Hey. You can look it up!"

THAT DAY WE FOUND
THE HUMMINGBIRD

Maryalice Plunkett was the ragamuffin new kid, under-sized, ratty clothes, self-important. "It's not Mary. Alice. You pronounce it, 'Mary-a-lease,' dummy." Some-times she acted like she hated everyone in school. But at the blackboard, she solved arithmetic problems faster than anyone in fifth grade.

Julia Brave Bull was Lakota. She lived next door with her mom and dad, unusual in 1950s Scottsbluff, Nebraska. We thought most Indians lived on reservations, were poor, and were not smart in school. But Julia dressed like a princess. She made straight A's.

Then there was me, Johnny Doonan. Not known for much of anything except my tendency to swear like a muleskinner, which I did frequently and loudly. Parents discouraged their children from playing with me.

So. For one reason or another, the three of us were out-siders, the rejects—the nerds, as a later era would have labeled us. We called ourselves The Mongoose Kids, after Rikki-Tikki-Tavi, the fierce little creature who fought the cobras in the Kipling story. We saw ourselves as standing together against a mean and toxic world.

Chance landed us at the same table for our library days. The other kids snickered at us. Sometimes they looked at us and twirled their index fingers at their heads. We didn't care. We had our own business. Much of it had to do with Plunkett's science fair project. She proposed to prove that ruby-throated hummingbirds came to western Nebraska. Some famous bird-watcher spoke to our class one day. She ridiculed Plunkett's notion. "Oh, I'm afraid not, honey." Plunkett simmered in her seat. I could see her little frame expand. She looked like a balloon ready to pop. "Well, then, I'll show you," Plunkett muttered.

Today she prowled through a new bird book, scowling and shaking her head.

"This book doesn't have much," she griped. "But look. See this range map? For the hummingbirds. It doesn't say ruby-throats specifically, but see those little wisps of shading? Sticking out from the main clump of the range? Yah, those little threads. I think they reach all the way out to here." I looked closely. Julia was trying to see across the table.

I said to Plunkett: "Well, that proves it, right? They come here. That's all you need, right?"

"Doonan, you don't get it. I have everything I need for a good science fair project. I know where hummingbirds go. I know how they breed. I drew a picture of what their nests look like. I know about their eggs. I have life-size pictures of hummingbirds so people can see how little they are compared to other things. Okay? I have poster board and wooden panels that I made with hinges. Everything. For a good science fair project. Get it? A good science fair project. What I want, I want the best, the most excellent champion science fair project Scottsbluff has ever seen. And if I can prove those ruby-throats come here, on my own. If I can prove that, it's original research with a scientific breakthrough. That's what I want."

It was the best speech I had ever heard anyone whisper.

Miss Jakes, the librarian, was looking our way, but she didn't seem stern. I risked a comment. "Like Doctor Salk with polio shots, right?"

"Not that important, Doonan. But it would be something new for people to know. It's important to contribute knowledge."

She stopped then, and her words held me frozen, her eyes radiating hot blue light straight into mine, and she looked away and looked down and sighed. "But I can't. I looked all over. Before it got cold. I looked all over to see if I could find one. I even know the flowers they like. I didn't see a one."

Julia was still staring across the table, first at Plunkett, then at Plunkett's book, then at me.

I plowed my mind, searching for something to say. For a suggestion, an idea, anything that would make Plunkett think I was smart and good and brave. I almost asked if she had tried looking in the cemetery, people brought flowers there all the time, and just before the words got out, I realized it was a dumb idea.

And then Julia spoke.

"I know where the hummingbird is."

Up snapped Plunkett's head. I stared like a dumb bunny. Plunkett jumped right on the point.

"Where?"

"I can show you," Julia said.

"Is it close?"

"We'll have to ride bikes." Julia looked right at me. She asked: "Can I borrow your extra one?" I was about to faint. I thought I'd fall out of my chair. Julia had lived next door for at least three years, and I saw her almost every day and she'd never spoken a word, and first she came to sit with us, and now we were having a conversation, and she wanted to use something I had.

She knew what was going on, that's for sure. For one thing, she knew that since Christmas, I'd had two bicycles.

"I guess. Sure. What about Plunkett?"

"Can you pump her on your new one?" I looked at Plunkett. She nodded. I said yes. This was going to be an adventure.

"We'll have to go on Saturday or Sunday. It might take all day," Julia said. "Where is it?" Plunkett asked again.

"Ma-a-pa-te," Julia said.

"What is that?" asked Plunkett.

"The big hill. On the other side of the river." She meant the Bluff. Our symbol. What our town was named after.

"That's where the hummingbird lives," Julia said.

***

The North Platte River was shallow and usually didn't move very fast. But crossing it meant you had to watch out for quicksand. All of us knew the stories about people getting pulled down out of sight, lost forever. Maybe they weren't true. Maybe our parents just told us to scare us away from the river. But the stories made me nervous just the same.

"Don't worry," said Julia. "I know the way."

We left our bikes in some bushes on the north bank and waded in. I carried a bag with some sandwiches and my Brownie box camera. Immediately my Levi's got wet up to the knees, and I could feel the river bottom squishing under my tennis shoes, but it wasn't sucking me down. Julia led, and Plunkett and I tried to follow exactly behind her.

The big bluff was so close now it was almost all I could see looking south. There was a road to the top on its other side. I had been there many times. You could see every town in the valley, and on a clear day, Laramie Peak poking up miles to the west in Wyoming.

Today I waded toward the bluff, and I felt very small. In PF Flyers and cuffed Levi's, I sloshed along the middle of a river that stretched clear across Nebraska. In front of me loomed a massive butte that had been there since the dinosaurs. It had helped keep the pioneers safe on the Oregon Trail. It had sheltered the trapper, Hiram Scott, who crawled there and died by its side. Julia told us her ancestors had fled to it for safety, like knights going to a castle.

I saw that it didn't have jagged edges like knives sticking out, or sharp pillars pointing up like Chimney Rock. It was high, long, and flat. The side facing us curved inward, like a spoon had scooped out a hollow for a resting place. I wondered if cave men had hidden there and used their fire to scare away saber-tooth tigers.

Daydreaming and gazing, I felt the river pulling high above my knees. I had wandered off the route Julia was forging and into deeper water. I felt the river bottom give way and its mud slurped at my ankle.

"Shit! I'm in the quicksand!" I yelled, threshing forward, arms flailing. I stumbled and the bottom of my pack with the sandwiches and the camera splashed. The canteen slipped off my other shoulder and started to float away. I grabbed it and lurched toward Plunkett and Julia.

"I'm sinking!"

I jerked my leg loose and fell forward with a flop and a splash, still trying to hold the food bag above water. The river soaked me. "Goddammit!" The girls waded over, and Plunkett grabbed the pack. Julia grabbed me by the wrists. "It's a good thing we're not fishing for anything," Julia said. "You'd scare everything away. And quit cussing. It's rude."

"What about that damn ... I mean that bird?" I asked.

"The hummingbird will be there, even with all your noise."

***

We crossed the river, and the achievement stunned me I had never done such a thing, nor come close to it. I looked back across the wide water and could not see the clump of bushes where we had hidden our bikes. We were in the wild. It had swallowed Scottsbluff and all its sound. Far above, a B-36 droned. It was the only noise we could hear. I looked up and spied the bomber, a tiny, silver cross high in the sky. It left a white vapor trail as it lumbered west from Omaha, and I wondered if it carried an atomic bomb.

The bluff towered over us. I craned away from the B-36 and looked straight up the butte wall, bending back my neck to see. It made me dizzy to stare at the top, and for one heart-beat I imagined the edge of it was starting to bulge out and topple on us. At my knee, a dragonfly hummed; I looked down and another bug made a clicking sound as it hopped from weed stalk to flower bud. The girls were so quiet, I thought they must have stopped breathing.

It was as if we had stepped through an invisible curtain and into another world.

Julia began walking, and without a word, Plunkett and I followed. We whisked through a blanket of sage and columbine, which Julia pointed out and named. Her science fair project was about plants, she said, and she showed us prairie gentian, its blue so pure and soft that I wanted to be one inch tall and burrow in its petals. I had never seen such a beautiful flower, or a shade of blue so powerful and perfect. I stopped and stared and thought that something magic must have colored it.

We walked up a hillock and down into a little hollow. We scared a meadowlark, its yellow chest flashing as it flew. We came to a willow tree. Soft grass and clover grew under it.

"Here," Julia said.

Plunkett looked around.

"Is this where the hummingbird is?"

"It will come," Julia answered. "We shouldn't think about it."

We sat.

Plunkett looked at my pack, damp from the river.

"I wonder if those sandwiches are all wet," she said.

They were soft and moist, but not from the river. I had made them with butter, peanut butter, and sweet pickles, and wrapped them in wax paper. Julia was suspicious, but Plunkett grabbed one and started munching. I passed around Cawley's potato chips. Julia decided to try a sandwich and after a bite or two, nodded approval. "Pretty good," she said. "Did your mother make them?"

"Nope. Me. Pickles don't make the bread all gooey like jelly does if you have to take them a long way. My aunt showed me how."

Julia and Plunkett seemed more impressed with that tip than they had been that time I told them I was going to box in a tournament for kids. There was no figuring girls.

We passed around the canteen and washed everything down. I took out my hunting knife and started throwing it into the ground like a mumblety-peg game.

I asked: "How many Mexicans d'ya think Davy Crockett killed at the Alamo before they got him?" The picture show had come out last year, but still I thought about it sometimes, and Fess Parker, the actor who played Davy, fighting like a hero at the end. I thought my question was a good one to discuss, kind of like a mystery.

"What difference does it make?" Julia said. "He's dead anyway. Like Custer."

I had read some books about Custer, and he was a hero in all of them. Julia didn't seem to think much of him.

I didn't want to start an argument, which I probably wouldn't win anyway. So I asked about the little spot where we rested. Plunkett was lying on her back, gazing at the clouds.

"We always come here," Julia said. "Unless the river is too high. My father said the only way you can get here is across the river the way we came. The first time, I was just a little girl."

"Do you have family picnics here?"

I was thinking about the big gatherings Mom's family had every year at Pioneer Park. We ate fried chicken and played softball and if it was close to the Fourth of July, shot off firecrackers. Or at least we shot them until my cousin stuffed a lit ladyfinger into his back pocket when he saw a policeman. It blew a hole in his pants and burned his butt, and now we weren't allowed to bring fireworks anymore, even sparklers.

"We come here for the peace and quiet," Julia said. "My mother, my father, me. My grandfather and grandmother before they died. It's where we come to talk about important things. I've never been here with anyone but them. And now you. And Plunkett."

For a few heartbeats, I thought about it. Julia had brought us to her family's special place. We weren't part of her family, but she showed it to us anyway. It made me want to be more polite and not cuss and quit talking about things like Davy Crockett killing Mexicans.

"My grandfather, and now my father, they tell the old stories. About our people coming here to hide from the soldiers. How they lived here for so long."

Julia looked right into my eyes for a few heartbeats. She started to say something, then shut her mouth, like she had changed her mind about talking. Then she talked anyway.

"My grandfather believed Wakan-tanka lived here. The Big Mystery. He thought this big hill had a spirit, like a ghost, and that it was good. He believed it watched us, kept us safe."

She stopped and looked at me like she expected me to laugh or make fun of her.

But I didn't say anything at all. I just looked at the bluff and nodded. Come to think of it, I felt pretty good sitting underneath it, like the bluff could take anything I worried about and make it disappear right into its old side.

Julia, eyes wide, spoke up.

"Look! The hummingbird. There's the hummingbird!"

***

It looked exactly the way Plunkett had described it.

The feathers on its back glistened as if they had been polished a deep green, and a bright red splash wrapped around its neck like a bandana. It was about three inches tall, and as the three of us loomed staring as it hovered over a flower, it showed not a speck of fear, nor even an awareness that humans watched.

"Oh. My. God. It's a ruby-throat, all right," Plunkett said. "Look at it! Oh, Doonan, get the camera! Quick!"

I ran for the pack and fumbled for the camera and hoped the water in the river hadn't gotten to the film. But the Brownie box had a tough hide, even if there was a damp stain on it. I twisted the film-winder to the first frame and tip-toed back to the bird.

The Brownie's lens made things look a mile away even if you were just shooting something in your yard, so I crept up as close as I could.

Six feet away, the ruby-throat still looked the size of a bee. I had to get closer.

"It's all right," Julia said. "He's busy. He won't even notice you. But hurry before he goes to another flower."

I got within three feet, then I dared two, and finally I held the camera not a foot away.

"Take it, take it!" Plunkett pleaded.

My thumb dragged down the little silver lever, the Brownie clicked, and the hummingbird pulled away from the flower about an inch, as if the noise had startled him. But then he went back to work.

I shoved the camera even closer and took another picture. Wow! I was doing real photography, like for a Boy Scout merit badge, and it was fun. I circled the flower and shot from another angle, and another and another. Once I got so close, I could see the bird's tiny black eyes glittering in the lens.

"See if you can hold him," Julia said to Plunkett. "Like this." She cupped her hands, fingers spread. "Don't squeeze, just make a little place for him. Don't shut your hands tight!"

Plunkett's hands formed a tiny cave. She eased it under the bird, pushing the flower away, and the ruby-throat fluttered inside her fingers. His wings beat so fast I could barely see them, and he danced in the tiny space, and he seemed to tilt his head and look right at Plunkett's face.

"Talk to him," Julia said. "Say something. He'll listen to you."

Plunkett did say something, but I couldn't make out the words. I was too busy backing and bending, twisting the film knob, and pulling the lever to take more pictures. I tried a couple of close-ups I hoped would show Plunkett and the bird both.

And then I ran out of film. Just as I did, the hummingbird burst out of Plunkett's fingers and shot straight up in the sky. He soared toward the top of the bluff, turned into a speck, and vanished.

Astonished, Plunkett rolled her eyes and threw her head back.

"Oh. My. God." she said. "Did you see that? I held him. Oh. My. God." She spun around, flopped on the ground, sprawled on her back, eyes wide, mouth open.

"I knew it. I told you. I knew ruby-throats came here. Doonan, did you get pictures?"

"Sure," I said. "Lots. Every bit of my film. It's color, too." Julia just smiled.

✳✳✳

We sat under the willow tree, and stayed for many, many heartbeats, not laughing, not even talking very much. We were just kids, but we felt like something important had happened. For one thing, I thought, we had worked together and accomplished a goal.

"We were like a team today," I said. I thought it felt as good as winning a baseball game. I felt pretty satisfied.

"I think there's another reason why we came here. I can't tell what it is, but my heart says something brought us here for it. Wakan-tanka, maybe," Julia said.

I knew that Julia liked to get mysterious once in a while. I looked at the bluff, then back at her. In a way, she was making things a little spooky, like the day I first saw the painting of Our Lady of Guadalupe in Mikey Sanchez's house. And then that made me think of the words they said in Mikey's church.

(... maker of heaven and earth,
of all that is, seen and unseen ...)

I said: "We're friends. Us three, we're the Mongoose Kids.

We're together, right? It's like we're the same. Like we're just supposed to be together."

What I wanted was to break the moody spell and maybe make all of us laugh, but the words didn't come out right, and instead all I thought of were more church words:

(... of one Being with the Father ...)

Then Plunkett said: "Well, it was the hummingbird, right? We had to find the hummingbird. That's why we came here."

(... all things were made
For us and our salvation ...)

And then all of a sudden, Plunkett did what I wanted. She got silly. She started giggling.

"We found it! We found the hummingbird, oh, you two! Oh, Julia, thank you! And Doonan, you got pictures to prove it!" And then, as if she were embarrassed for saying it all, she scooped up a whole handful of dirt and, giggling even louder, dumped it all over my head.

It made me mad, a little. But I saw Plunkett laughing as she grabbed another handful and tossed it on Julia. I scooped up my own and leaned over and rubbed it in Plunkett's hair. Then Julia started laughing and jumped on us both and in a heartbeat the three of us were wrestling and throwing soil and getting it in our ears and our noses and down our necks. Somehow the foolishness brought us even closer, as if with those handfuls of dirt, we had baptized ourselves into a friendship that would last forever.

We got filthy, and we laughed until we couldn't breathe. I couldn't remember laughing so hard. I couldn't remember being so happy. Our laughter finally softened, drifting away until only our smiles remained. I asked Plunkett what she said to the hummingbird.

"I told him I loved him. And … I told him … I love you guys, too."

(… world without end … Amen.)

NEBRASKA CORNFIELD

On one green stalk
A daddy longlegs
Pulls step by reaching step,
a scribble, nothing more,
moving toward the light.
In a whispering cornfield forest
A child entranced scouts so far within
that the rush of a soil-scent wind
becomes the only voice other than his own
humming gently Sweet Afton,
and each note rising alone.
A leg—no, a thread, trembling.
The child stares, hand high to hit, to crush,
because who, after all,
in that forest is there to say don't?
A heartbeat, a shadow, a step.
Two go their way.
One toward the light.
The other alone.

THE CATS OF SECASTILLA

My father was a violent man. He liked to slap my mother, especially when he drank. One day she pulled a pistol. She fired twice, missing him. Bullets hit the wall and ceiling. Debris fell into my crib. My mother's cat, which she called Poosay, jumped in and pressed against me. I hugged it and pushed my face into its fur. My father ran out the door. I never saw him again. Mother told me this story many times. She said it was why I loved cats, calling it an infantile memory of sweet comfort. I suppose that could be true. Years later, a therapist told me the episode spawned my travel affliction, a never-ending desire to flit from one destination to another. It was akin to a grail quest, the analyst said, and my vanished father was the holy goal. What a load of nonsense. I traveled because I was a travel writer, sending dispatches to newspapers and airline magazines about unusual destinations.

It was why I came to Spain. To Graus. It was how I met Daisy. It was where I met the cats of Secastilla, and where I recognized, at last, the meaning of loss, loyalty, redemption, and love.

***

I asked the editor: "Why not send me to San Sebastian? Even Pamplona. I could join the running of the fools."

"You mean the bulls," the editor said, not catching the joke. "And no. You are too old. The bulls would catch you and you would be *muerto*. Dead, you know."

"And your point is?"

"Do you think you are Hemingway?"

"No. I am better."

"Then go to Graus. Turn it into the jewel of España. Show us how good you are."

I stalked out. Didn't answer. Left the editor's challenge hanging. But she knew she had me. Editors can be clever like that.

*****

I checked flights, drove to the airport in Tampa, and parked in long term. Caught the plane to Spain. Yes, the words to *that* song hummed through my head. In flight, I sang them after several glasses of Wither Hills Sauvignon Blanc 2013. The smiling steward put a finger to his lips. He was pretty cute.

"Are you gay?" I asked.

"I believe I am straight," he said. "But as John Lennon famously said, perhaps the right man has not come along. You are not he."

Shattered again. I took an Ambien and went to sleep. I hope I snored.

✳✳✳

Woke up with a headache and a sense of the surreal. Apparently, I rented a car in Barcelona. I didn't come to until I was halfway to Graus on the A 2. When I arrived, I took an apartment at the Hotel Lleida. I also noted that I had forgotten to retrieve my duffel at the airport. Ah well, perhaps they will give my clothing to the poor. I flopped on the bed. I heard a scratching at my door and a dissonant moan. I had no device to measure the wave-geometry properties, but guessed the call rose from an A to a C-sharp on the middle C octave. It suggested a sad cat's presence, but when I opened the door, no cat was present.

✳✳✳

Gunfire, singing, and marching bands awakened me at 8 a.m. My apartment looked out on Calle Salamero, the main street, where a parade moved along far too slowly. Tall puppets wearing robes and crowns glided on stilts. Other marchers wore artificial, round heads the size of tractor wheels. They waved to people leaning out their apartment windows. The people waved back. When the procession reached my window, I glowered down. 8 a.m.! Some kind of bagpipes! Many men carried black-powder blunderbusses. They discharged them often, and the stout reports rattled my window. Children threw firecrackers. I later learned this was a festival day. It was the kind of local color the editor wanted. I did not. I wanted a beer and needed new clothes. My trousers stood on their own. The front of my shirt re-sembled a purée. Apparently, I had tried to eat a pizza some time back. I could recall no such meal. But I believed in lost time, or what the hoi-polloi call blackouts.

***

Outside, I stroked free-style through a belly-to-buttocks crowd. I saw an orange cat, unperturbed, sitting as if on a throne. It guarded a bar's doorway. It held my gaze for a mo-ment, then with the elegance of a danseur, rose and pranced inside. I had no choice but to follow. The bar boasted three deep, but I immediately caught the tender's eye. It must have been my patrician bearing suggesting a fellow who would tolerate no nonsense.

"La cerveza mas grande que tienes," I bellowed. Unsmil-ing patrons turned to see. "Tengo muy thirsty," I explained. The tender stepped to the Estrella tap and filled a vessel slightly smaller than a bucket. "Un Euro cincuenta. Fiesta especial," he said. I grasped the bucket and began to drink. The beer was cold. It was lovable. Its essence filled my nose and throat. Five seconds, ten, fifteen, on I guzzled. The pa-trons began to slap the bar in rhythm to my bobbing Adam's apple. Now I was invincible, the super-hero Lung Man, I could hold my breath longer than a Navy SEAL. Down went the final dribble. I gasped, wiped my mouth, fell against the wall, and took a bow. Someone shouted. "Un incondicianal!

El Americano eccentrico!" I learned later it was a polite way of saying "what a headcase." I wondered how they knew I was an American.

＊＊＊

Off to the men's store. The proprietor measured me shoulder to shoulder, crotch to toe. He got in my face to measure my neck, turning away sharply when I exhaled. I bought a white shirt so bright it made my eyes water. It had pre-rolled cuffs with cunning blue stripes. I had to have the snowy trousers with pleats in front. I added a gray, felt fedora. Finally, a pair of black half-boots with zippers up the sides. I stood in front of a mirror. "My god," I said. "Magnifico." Relieved, the proprietor nodded. Outside, I saw an orange cat. "You again? Or are you someone's brother." It followed me back, waiting patiently at the bar while I had another bucket.

＊＊＊

This procedure I followed for several days. A bucket, followed by the men's store. At first the proprietor cast down his eyes when I stepped in. His attitude improved as I depleted his inventory. I acquired a tower of trousers in the basic colors and shirts of all descriptions: solids, stripes, paisley (which reminded me of my youth), button-downs, and batwings. All of the wardrobe I would add to my expense account. A man must dress, after all. The cat seemed to have gone away, as cats, being transitory creatures, will do. After a week, my routine bored me. I wondered if I was drifting toward expatriate decadence. It was not pretty to think so, as Hemingway didn't say. I took long walks to discourage dissipation. I thought I would like crossing the bridge over the Esera River, hiking all the way to the Albergue de Graus, a hostel for tourists without expense accounts, probably featuring bunk beds and eight to a room. Fitting for barbarians; they likely were the stocking-cap sort who put slick wooden slabs on their feet and attempted to slide down menacing slopes. Fine. Perhaps the exercise would diminish their numbers.

****

My attitude became my armor. My razor and the shower knobs stayed still. I gazed at dark hills huddling near the town. I suppose some would call them atmospheric, haunting Spanish geography, mountains of mystery. I called them depressing. Bah. No doubt Iberian cougars lurked, poised to leap upon and chew without mercy an unwary rambler. I wandered often to the river, a pleasant and tempting stream. One day I paused on the bridge. Why, oh why, did I come here. The water below sighed over dark boulders. *Here we wait, waifs who want you within, when will you wet your whey-face.* Foot on a rail, yes, I thought of leaping. (Hold on there, soldier. Nope. Right face ... forward march ... go to your left, your right, your left ... and so on.)

I resumed my daily routine, which included Xanax and beer. Here I insert a disclaimer: Be careful with that stuff. At a sidewalk café, my Spanish dictionary always at hand, I perused *Alto Aragón* and *El País*. Scribbled in a notebook. Began a novel, which ended after two paragraphs. Read querulous emails from the editor. What are you doing? Are you even there? Why haven't you filed? I typed back: Still researching. Thank you for the note. It reminds me that I must go to the men's room and make your doppelganger.

One day at that same sidewalk café, I sipped a head-clearing espresso. An orange cat passed. It lunged at a sparrow, missing and disappearing halfway under a Peugeot parked nose in. I for some reason rose, bent, and grasped the cat at its belly. I hugged it to my chest. It squirmed to its back and glared. "Hola, gato," I said tactfully, aware of fang and claw.

"Thank you?"

A rising voice, maybe a G note to an A above middle C. I glanced up, side to side, down. I spied a woman, then a leash she held, bereft of its animal. I began to reinsert the writhing beast, doing a poor job of it. Toe to top, the woman wore black velvet ballet flats, white hose, a pink dress with white flowers, and a little straw bonnet with a lavender band. She had a pink and blue purse. Distracted, I continued to fumble the cat. To my level the woman lowered. I saw reddish-blonde hair, and wide eyes, blue like the blue in a flame.

"You must be El Americano Eccentrico?" she said.

"I, um, sí."

"They call me La Dama Loca de los Gatos? The Crazy Cat Lady? You may call me Daisy if you like?"

"Claro," I said.

"Would you prefer to speak English?"

"Claro," I repeated. "Of course, I mean. Of course."

"May I buy you lunch? To say thank you? For catching the cat? Would your wife mind?"

I told her I was alone. No wife. Asked about her husband.

"He hated my cats? If he saw a new one around the door, he ... he would stamp on its head? Then he would hit me?"

"So I poisoned him? They said it seemed to be a heart attack?"

***

Over a lunch of scrambled eggs and longaniza, she said: "I wonder what your name is?"

"Doonan, John. John. Doonan." The master of redundancy, I.

"I will call you Johnson?" Daisy said.

I liked it, despite its mildly salacious connotation, or perhaps because of it.

"You must come to see my cats?" she said.

***

Daisy drove. I held the cat in my lap. "Her name is Mishu," Daisy said. "It means faithful and honest. Sometimes she comes down the mountain. By herself into town. She always comes back.”

“You came with her today.”

“Yes. She is a very intelligent creature, but she has not learned to shop and spend money on her own. We went to the Fresh Mercados. She always chooses her own food. Today it was ham.”

I noticed that out of Graus, Daisy spoke in the declarative rather than the interrogative.

“I am nervous there. Uncertain. I worry about the *guardia civil*,” she said. “I worry that they suspect me. Because I poisoned him, you see.”

I said nothing. I decided to be very polite.

***

Up a hill, around a curve, we entered Secastilla. It was a compact village. A maze of narrow streets connected its orange-yellow dwellings, two and three stories tall. Quiet as a church. I took a deep breath. First one in a while, I thought.

A bundle of sprawling cats lay outside Daisy’s door. “I have fourteen,” she said. “But only six live inside. Strays.”

She took my hand and led me to the bedroom. She stepped out of her velvet ballets, pulled off the white stockings, and turned her back to me. “Please,” she said. I unzipped her dress. She pulled it off, revealing a silken slip. “Lie down,” she said. She got beside me and rubbed my head until I fell asleep. I remember glasses of water. One, then another and another. But always I drifted off. And off, again and again. When I awakened, I could tweak my beard between thumb and forefinger.

"You were very sick," Daisy said. "The drink, I suspect. But also, a long sadness whose source I can only guess."

"How is it you can say so? You don't know me."

"Johnson, do you believe in God?"

"I don't know. Not especially, I guess. You?"

"No. I never could. But I tried praying. There were cats."

"You prayed about cats?"

"No. I prayed because of them. They knew my secrets. They still came to me. I think they loved me. I think they do. I wanted to be a better person for them."

"You believe I have a long sadness."

"Yes. I see yours as I see my own."

****

"I need to shave," I said. "And may I bathe?"

****

Afterward, I tore my heart open, and Daisy hers to me. I told her I was mediocre, a hack writer, a drunk, a liar. "You know I am a murderess," she said. "You cannot trust me. Cross me and I will bury you in my arbor."

Yet I heard our bladed words as if they were gliding arpeggios. My throat tightened and my eyes began to swell. I had to step outside. I looked at the bundle of cats, immovable and everlasting.

"Hola, mis hermanos," I said. I gazed at the welcoming hills. I wished good hunting for the Iberian cougars. I blessed the stocking-cap skiers and prayed for them a glorious day. My acid fell away and my armor crumbled to rust.

✳✳✳

I asked to use Daisy's laptop. I played a game of solitaire, my fingers wandering over the dusty keyboard. I spoke to it as an old friend long unseen. "Perhaps you no longer know me," I said. I began to type. At the top I put a title.

The Jewel of España.

At last, I knew what it meant.

THE BOUT

Pounding like fireworks
Rolling over water,
Fists in gloves
Tear my cheek,
Crush my nose.
How odd to hear
But not to Feel
Death,
One touch at a time.

What ancient hatred?
I did not know its name.
Nor can I say it yet.
But its poison let me stand
When god! I wanted to run and fall.

When it was done
And the Blows had gone
Quiet like heavy chords
Lost in hallelujah shouting,
I kissed the bruises
Sweet on my skin,
For in that moment
Nothing I imagined
Could hurt any more.

Now my grandson sleeps.
On my chest I feel him breathe.
On my soft jaw
I feel his tiny fist.
My soul at last is rested.

... FAREWELL

Geography leaves its signature in every soul. I still feel close to the austere and ancient landscape I first knew: the spires and domes and the mighty bluff overlooking the North Platte River Valley. I think of them not as careless piles of rock but as castles and cathedrals and dolmens, each inhabited by a spirit of its own. I think of the ruts of the Oregon Trail, and how on all fours I crept in the olden tracks, a child exploring history, and the prairie brambles that scratched my fingers were the seedlings of those that tangled in the wheels of the pioneer wagons west ...

... I would tell you of the gentle Gulf of Mexico, its summer surf pushing a rope of foam over the feet of two kids dizzy from their first open-mouth kiss ...

... I would speak of towering cottonwoods, tilled and irrigated farmland spread mile over verdant square mile, row after row of beets and beans and corn, green and constant and comforting even as the coyote crying at night warns us: Do not boast, you are not so far from the wilderness and the skeleton fields of winter ...

... And I would ask you to know the dreadnaught surge

of desperate tropical water crushing dwellings and dreams to kindling …

… The land and the sea teach beauty and brutality, and their moods leave magic in the human heart, guiding its endless search for new ways to see, new ways to know, new answers to mysteries …

This book's stories, poems, and essay speak of passion, love, loss, loyalty, and inspiration. They speak of friendship, grief, and redemption. There is an implied element of quest. We search for something more than ourselves, if not a god or savior, then certainly a higher value. Perhaps we simply seek a journey that will make us better human beings. Sometimes we find it. Sometimes we fail. Sometimes we are merely helpless at the gates of Graceland …

… And there, with innocence lost, we seek another path to follow.

Gradatim ferociter,
Jon
2025

ACKNOWLEDGMENTS

I did not write *Helpless at the Gates of Graceland* alone. People of great heart and spirit pitched in to improve the manuscript and help create this book. I thank St. Petersburg Press publisher Amy Cianci. She believed in the book from the start and gracefully guided it through the stages of production. I thank artist Justin Groom, whose work unerringly captured the mood of the book itself and the pieces therein. Thanks go to proofreader Amy M. Kagan, whose needle-eyed diligence sharpened my prose and smoothed its flow. To Becky Day Wilson, my wife: thank you, thank you, thank you. She endured my flights of fancy and listened to my dark muttering with grace and patience and humor. In short: What an extraordinary team!

AUTHOR'S NOTES

"Jesus Up the Creek": One day I saw an old music box in Brocante Vintage Market on 22nd Street South in St. Petersburg. It played a widely recognized hymn. On the inside of its lid was a name: Jenny. When I saw it, the story spooled out of my head as if waiting to be released.

"Lyric for Love": There is mystery about the cliffs of Dooneen. Some have said they are mythical. There has been discussion about where exactly in Ireland they are located. Christy Moore offers a lovely tribute. You can find the Irish folksinger on the Internet, as you can Planxty, a group he helped found. The cliffs are a geographic reality. They are also a place in the heart.

ABOUT THE AUTHOR

Helpless at the Gates of Graceland represents a departure for Jon Wilson, whose six previous books have focused on local history. Wilson has lived in St. Petersburg since 1956. He worked as a reporter and editor for 37 years for the *Tampa Bay Times* and *Evening Independent,* and 11 years for Florida Humanities. He holds a bachelor's degree in English and master's degrees in Journalism Studies and in Liberal Arts, all from the University of South Florida St. Petersburg.